D0097673

THE OUTING

The Outing

A STORY BY DYLAN THOMAS
with illustrations by Meg Stevens

J. M. Dent   London

First published in the volume
A Prospect of the Sea
under the title 'A Story' in 1955.
First published in this edition 1971
Reprinted 1972, 1974, 1975, 1978, 1982, 1985, 1990, 1994

Text © the Trustees for the Copyrights of Dylan Thomas 1954
Illustrations © J. M. Dent & Sons Ltd 1971

All rights reserved. No part of this publication may be
reproduced, stored in a retrieval system, or transmitted, in any
form or by any means, electronic, mechanical, photocopying,
recording or otherwise, without the prior permission of
J. M. Dent & Sons Ltd.

Printed in Italy

THE OUTING

THE OUTING: A STORY

If you can call it a story. There's no real beginning or end and there's very little in the middle. It is all about a day's outing, by charabanc, to Porthcawl, which, of course, the charabanc never reached, and it happened when I was so high and much nicer.

I was staying at the time with my uncle and his wife. Although she was my aunt, I never thought of her as anything but the wife of my uncle, partly because he was so big and trumpeting and red-hairy and used to fill every inch of the hot little house like an old buffalo squeezed into an airing cupboard, and partly because she was so small and silk and quick and made no noise at all as she whisked about on padded paws, dusting the china dogs, feeding the buffalo, setting the mousetraps that never caught her; and once she sleaked out of the room, to squeak in a nook or nibble in the hayloft, you forgot she had ever been there.

But there he was, always, a steaming hulk of an uncle, his braces straining like hawsers, crammed behind the counter of the tiny shop at the front of the house, and breathing like a brass band; or guzzling and blustery in the kitchen over his gutsy supper, too big for every-thing except the great black boats of his boots. As he ate, the house grew smaller; he billowed out over the furniture, the loud check meadow of his waistcoat littered, as though after a picnic, with cigarette ends, peelings, cabbage stalks, birds' bones, gravy; and the forest fire of his hair crackled among the hooked hams from the ceiling. She was so small she could hit him only if she stood on a chair, and every Saturday night at half past ten he would lift her up, under his arm, on

to a chair in the kitchen so that she could hit him on the head with whatever was handy, which was always a china dog. On Sundays, and when pickled, he sang high tenor, and had won many cups.

The first I heard of the annual outing was when I was sitting one evening on a bag of rice behind the counter, under one of my uncle's stomachs, reading an advertisement for sheep-dip, which was all there was to read. The shop was full of my uncle, and when Mr Benjamin Franklyn, Mr Weazley, Noah Bowen, and Will Sentry came in, I thought it would burst. It was like all being together in a drawer that smelt of cheese and turps, and twist tobacco and sweet biscuits and snuff and waistcoat. Mr Benjamin Franklyn said that he had collected enough money for the charabanc and twenty cases of pale ale and a pound apiece over that he would distribute among the members of the outing when they first stopped for refreshment, and he was about sick and tired, he said, of being followed by Will Sentry.

'All day long, wherever I go,' he said, 'he's after me like a collie with one eye. I got a shadow of my own *and* a dog. I don't need no Tom, Dick, or Harry pursuing me with his dirty muffler on.'

Will Sentry blushed, and said: 'It's only oily. I got a bicycle.'

'A man has no privacy at all,' Mr Franklyn went on.
'I tell you he sticks so close I'm afraid to go out the
back in case I sit in his lap. It's a wonder to me,' he
said, 'he don't follow me into bed at night.'

'Wife won't let,' Will Sentry said.

And that started Mr Franklyn off again, and they tried
to soothe him down by saying: 'Don't you mind Will
Sentry' ... 'No harm in old Will' ... 'He's only
keeping an eye on the money, Benjie.'

'Aren't I honest?' asked Mr Franklyn in surprise.
There was no answer for some time, then Noah Bowen

said: 'You know what the committee is. Ever since Bob the Fiddle they don't feel safe with a new treasurer.'

'Do you think *I*'m going to drink the outing funds, like Bob the Fiddle did?' said Mr Franklyn.

'You *might*,' said my uncle slowly.

'I resign,' said Mr Franklyn.

'Not with our money you won't,' Will Sentry said.

'Who put dynamite in the salmon pool?' said Mr Weazley, but nobody took any notice of him. And, after a time, they all began to play cards in the thickening dusk of the hot, cheesy shop, and my uncle blew and bugled whenever he won, and Mr Weazley grumbled like a dredger, and I fell to sleep on the gravy-scented mountain meadow of uncle's waistcoat.

On Sunday evening, after Bethesda, Mr Franklyn walked into the kitchen where my uncle and I were eating sardines with spoons from the tin because it was Sunday and his wife would not let us play draughts.

She was somewhere in the kitchen, too. Perhaps she was inside the grandmother clock, hanging from the weights and breathing. Then, a second later, the door

opened again and Will Sentry edged into the room, twiddling his hard, round hat. He and Mr Franklyn sat down on the settee, stiff and moth-balled and black in their chapel and funeral suits.

'I brought the list,' said Mr Franklyn. 'Every member fully paid. You ask Will Sentry.'

My uncle put on his spectacles, wiped his whiskery mouth with a handkerchief big as a Union Jack, laid down his spoon of sardines, took Mr Franklyn's list of names, removed the spectacles so that he could read, and then ticked the names off one by one.

'Enoch Davies. Aye. He's good with his fists. You never know. Little Gerwain. Very melodious bass. Mr Cadwalladwr. That's right. He can tell opening time better than my watch. Mr Weazley. Of course. He's been to Paris. Pity he suffers so much in the charabanc. Stopped us nine times last year between the Beehive and the Red Dragon. Noah Bowen, ah, very peaceable. He's got a tongue like a turtle-dove. Never a argument with Noah Bowen. Jenkins Loughor. Keep him off economics. It cost us a plate-glass window. And ten pints for the Sergeant. Mr Jervis. Very tidy.'

'He tried to put a pig in the charra,' Will Sentry said.

'Live and let live,' said my uncle.

Will Sentry blushed.

'Sinbad the Sailor's Arms. Got to keep in with him. Old O. Jones.'

'Why old O. Jones?' said Will Sentry.

'Old O. Jones always goes,' said my uncle.

I looked down at the kitchen table. The tin of sardines was gone. By Gee, I said to myself, Uncle's wife is quick as a flash.

'Cuthbert Johnny Fortnight. Now there's a card,' said my uncle.

'He whistles after women,' Will Sentry said.

'So do you,' said Mr Benjamin Franklyn, 'in your mind.'

My uncle at last approved the whole list, pausing only to say, when he came across one name: 'If we weren't a Christian community, we'd chuck that Bob the Fiddle in the sea.'

'We can do that in Porthcawl,' said Mr Franklyn, and soon after that he went, Will Sentry no more than an inch behind him, their Sunday-bright boots squeaking on the kitchen cobbles.

And then, suddenly, there was my uncle's wife standing in front of the dresser, with a china dog in one hand. By Gee, I said to myself again, did you ever see such a woman, if that's what she is. The lamps were not lit yet in the kitchen and she stood in a wood of shadows, with the plates on the dresser behind her shining—like pink-and-white eyes.

'If you go on that outing on Saturday, Mr Thomas,' she said to my uncle in her small, silk voice, 'I'm going home to my mother's.'

Holy Mo, I thought, she's got a mother. Now that's one old bald mouse of a hundred and five I won't be wanting to meet in a dark lane.

'It's me or the outing, Mr Thomas.'

I would have made my choice at once, but it was almost half a minute before my uncle said: 'Well, then, Sarah, it's the outing, my love.' He lifted her up, under his arm, on to a chair in the kitchen, and she hit him

on the head with the china dog. Then he lifted her down again, and then I said good night.

For the rest of the week my uncle's wife whisked quiet and quick round the house with her darting duster, my uncle blew and bugled and swole, and I kept myself busy all the time being up to no good. And then at breakfast time on Saturday morning, the morning of the outing, I found a note on the kitchen table. It said: 'There's some eggs in the pantry. Take your boots off before you go to bed.' My uncle's wife had gone, as quick as a flash.

When my uncle saw the note, he tugged out the flag of his handkerchief and blew such a hubbub of trumpets that the plates on the dresser shook. 'It's the same every year,' he said. And then he looked at me. 'But this year it's different. *You*'ll have to come on the outing, too, and what the members will say I dare not think.'

The charabanc drew up outside, and when the members of the outing saw my uncle and me squeeze out of the shop together, both of us cat-licked and brushed in our Sunday best, they snarled like a zoo.

'Are you bringing a *boy*?' asked Mr Benjamin Franklyn as we climbed into the charabanc. He looked at me with horror.

'Boys is nasty,' said Mr Weazley.

'He hasn't paid his contributions,' Will Sentry said.

'No room for boys. Boys get sick in charabancs.'

'So do you, Enoch Davies,' said my uncle.

'Might as well bring *women*.'

The way they said it, women were worse than boys.

'Better than bringing grandfathers.'

'Grandfathers is nasty too,' said Mr Weazley.

'What can we do with him when we stop for refresh-ments?'

'I'm a grandfather,' said Mr Weazley.

'Twenty-six minutes to opening time,' shouted an old man in a panama hat, not looking at a watch. They forgot me at once.

'Good old Mr Cadwalladwr,' they cried, and the charabanc started off down the village street.

A few cold women stood at their doorways, grimly watching us go. A very small boy waved good-bye, and his mother boxed his ears. It was a beautiful August morning.

We were out of the village, and over the bridge, and up the hill towards Steeplehat Wood when Mr Franklyn, with his list of names in his hand, called out loud: 'Where's old O. Jones?'

'Where's old O?'

'We've left old O behind.'

'Can't go without old O.'

And though Mr Weazley hissed all the way, we turned and drove back to the village, where, outside the Prince of Wales, old O. Jones was waiting patiently and alone with a canvas bag.

'I didn't want to come at all,' old O. Jones said as they hoisted him into the charabanc and clapped him on the back and pushed him on a seat and stuck a bottle in his hand, 'but I always go.' And over the bridge and up the hill and under the deep green wood and along

the dusty road we wove, slow cows and ducks flying by, until 'Stop the bus!' Mr Weazley cried. 'I left my teeth on the mantelpiece.'

'Never you mind,' they said, 'you're not going to bite nobody,' and they gave him a bottle with a straw.

'I might want to smile,' he said.

'Not you,' they said.

'What's the time, Mr Cadwalladwr?'

'Twelve minutes to go,' shouted back the old man in the panama, and they all began to curse him.

The charabanc pulled up outside the Mountain Sheep, a small, unhappy public-house with a thatched roof like a wig with ringworm. From a flagpole by the Gents fluttered the flag of Siam. I knew it was the flag of Siam because of cigarette cards. The landlord stood at the door to welcome us, simpering like a wolf. He was a long, lean, black-fanged man with a greased love-curl and pouncing eyes. 'What a beautiful August day!' he said, and touched his love-curl with a claw. That was the way he must have welcomed the Mountain Sheep before he ate it, I said to myself. The members rushed out, bleating, and into the bar.

'You keep an eye on the charra,' my uncle said; 'see nobody steals it now.'

'There's nobody to steal it,' I said, 'except some cows,' but my uncle was gustily blowing his bugle in the bar.

I looked at the cows opposite, and they looked at me. There was nothing else for us to do. Forty-five minutes passed, like a very slow cloud. The sun shone down on the lonely road, the lost, unwanted boy, and the lake eyed cows. In the dark bar they were so happy they were breaking glasses. A Shoni-Onion Breton man, with a beret and a necklace of onions, bicycled down the road and stopped at the door.

'Quelle un grand matin, monsieur,' I said.

'There's French, boy bach!' he said.

I followed him down the passage, and peered into the bar. I could hardly recognize the members of the outing. They had all changed colour. Beetroot, rhubarb, and puce, they hollered and rollicked in that dark, damp hole like enormous ancient bad boys, and my uncle surged in the middle, all red whiskers and bellies. On the floor was broken glass and Mr Weazley.

'Drinks all round,' cried Bob the Fiddle, a small, absconding man with bright blue eyes and a plump smile.

'Who's been robbing the orphans?'

'Who's sold his little babby to the gyppoes?'

'Trust old Bob, he'll let you down.'

'You will have your little joke,' said Bob the Fiddle,
smiling like a razor, 'but I forgive you, boys.'

Out of the fug and babel I heard: 'Come out and
fight.'

'No, not now, later.'

'No, now when I'm in a temper.'

'Look at Will Sentry, he's proper snobbled.'

'Look at his wilful feet.'

'Look at Mr Weazley lording it on the floor.'

Mr Weazley got up, hissing like a gander. 'That boy pushed me down deliberate,' he said, pointing to me at the door, and I slunk away down the passage and out to the mild, good cows. Time clouded over, the cows wondered, I threw a stone at them and they wandered, wondering, away. Then out blew my uncle, ballooning, and one by one the members lumbered after him in a grizzle. They had drunk the Mountain Sheep dry. Mr Weazley had won a string of onions that the Shoni Onion man raffled in the bar. 'What's the good of onions if you left your teeth on the mantelpiece?' he said. And when I looked through the back window of the thundering charabanc, I saw the pub grow smaller in the distance. And the flag of Siam, from the flagpole by the Gents, fluttered now at half mast.

The Blue Bull, the Dragon, the Star of Wales, the Twll in the Wall, the Sour Grapes, the Shepherd's Arms, the Bells of Aberdovey: I had nothing to do in

the whole, wild August world but remember the
names where the outing stopped and keep an eye on
the charabanc. And whenever it passed a public⹁

house, Mr Weazley would cough like a billygoat and
cry: 'Stop the bus, I'm dying of breath!' And back
we would have to go.

Closing time meant nothing to the members of that
outing. Behind locked doors, they hymned and rum⹁
pused all the beautiful afternoon. And, when a police⹁

man entered the Druid's Tap by the back door, and found them all choral with beer, 'Sssh!' said Noah Bowen, 'the pub is shut.'

'Where do you come from?' he said in his buttoned, blue voice.

They told him.

'I got a auntie there,' the policeman said. And very soon he was singing 'Asleep in the Deep.'

Off we drove again at last, the charabanc bouncing with tenors and flagons, and came to a river that rushed along among willows.

'Water!' they shouted.

'Porthcawl!' sang my uncle.

'Where's the donkeys?' said Mr Weazley.

And out they lurched, to paddle and whoop in the cool, white, winding water. Mr Franklyn, trying to polka on the slippery stones, fell in twice. 'Nothing is simple,' he said with dignity as he oozed up the bank.

'It's cold!' they cried.

'It's lovely!'

'It's smooth as a moth's nose!'

'It's *better* than Porthcawl!'

And dusk came down warm and gentle on thirty wild, wet, pickled, splashing men without a care in the world at the end of the world in the west of Wales.

And, 'Who goes there?' called Will Sentry to a wild duck flying.

They stopped at the Hermit's Nest for a rum to keep out the cold. 'I played for Aberavon in 1898,' said a stranger to Enoch Davies.

'Liar,' said Enoch Davies.

'I can show you photos,' said the stranger.

'Forged,' said Enoch Davies.

'And I'll show you my cap at home.'

'Stolen.'

'I got friends to prove it,' the stranger said in a fury.

'Bribed,' said Enoch Davies.

On the way home, through the simmering moon-splashed dark, old O. Jones began to cook his supper on a primus stove in the middle of the charabanc. Mr Weazley coughed himself blue in the smoke. 'Stop the

bus,' he cried, 'I'm dying of breath!' We all climbed
down into the moonlight. There was not a public-
house in sight. So they carried out the remaining cases,
and the primus stove, and old O. Jones himself, and
took them into a field, and sat down in a circle in the
field and drank and sang while O. Jones cooked
sausage and mash and the moon flew above us. And
there I drifted to sleep against my uncle's mountainous
waistcoat, and, as I slept, 'Who goes there?' called out
Will Sentry to the flying moon.